BONNIE BRYANT

PONY TAILS™

Jasmine Trots Ahead

BANTAM BOOKS
TORONTO · NEW YORK · LONDON · SYDNEY · AUCKLAND

JASMINE TROTS AHEAD
A BANTAM BOOK : 0 553 505084

First published in USA by Skylark Books,
a division of Bantam Doubleday Dell Publishing Group, Inc.

First publication in Great Britain

PRINTING HISTORY
Bantam edition published 1997

Set in 14/16pt Linotype New Century Schoolbook by
Phoenix Typesetting, Ilkley, West Yorkshire

Bantam Books are published by Transworld Publishers Ltd,
61–63 Uxbridge Road, Ealing, London W5 5SA,
in Australia by Transworld Publishers (Australia) Pty. Ltd,
15–25 Helles Avenue, Moorebank, NSW 2170,
and in New Zealand by Transworld Publishers (NZ) Ltd,
3 William Pickering Drive, Albany, Auckland.

Printed and bound in Great Britain by
Cox & Wyman Ltd, Reading, Berkshire.

I would like to give my special thanks to Catherine Hapka for her help in the writing of this book.

1
THE HORSE WISE
MEETING

"I wonder what today's meeting is about," Jasmine James said.

"I don't know," said Corey Taka-mura. "Max didn't tell us last week."

It was Saturday morning. Jasmine, Corey, and their other best friend, May Grover, were waiting for their weekly Pony Club meeting to start. Their Pony Club was called Horse

Wise. It met at Pine Hollow Stables, where the three girls also took riding lessons. Max Regnery was the owner of Pine Hollow and their riding teacher. He was the head of their Pony Club, too.

This week's meeting was unmounted, which meant that Jasmine, May, and Corey had left their ponies at home. The three girls were neighbours, and they all kept their ponies in stables behind their houses. When the girls had mounted Horse Wise meetings, May's father brought their ponies to Pine Hollow in his horsebox.

"I hope this meeting isn't something boring like rolling bandages," May said.

Corey shrugged. "I don't even mind doing that," she said. "At least it still has something to do with ponies."

"That reminds me," Jasmine said, tucking a strand of her long blond hair back into its pony-tail. "I meant to tell you two about the model horse I saw when my mum and I were in the shopping centre yesterday. Or rather, the model *pony*." Jasmine loved model horses and had a big collection of them. May and Corey liked them, too, but they didn't have very many. That didn't matter, because Jasmine let them play with hers. It was part of being best friends. That was why the three girls called themselves the Pony Tails – they were best friends and they all loved ponies.

"A model pony?" Corey said. "What did it look like?"

"That's the best part," Jasmine said. "It looked just like Outlaw. It had the same kind of mask and every-thing." Outlaw was Jasmine's pony. He was dark brown except for a white mask on his face that made him look like an old-fashioned bank robber.

"It sounds perfect," May said. "You have to get it!"

"I know," Jasmine said. She sighed. "But it will take me for ever to save up enough from my pocket money. And Christmas is months and months away."

Just then a girl their age named Erin Mosley leaned over to talk to them. Erin had been taking lessons at Pine Hollow for almost a year, but she had just joined Horse Wise. "Why doesn't your mother just buy it for you?" Erin asked Jasmine. "My parents buy me anything I want. All I have to do is ask."

"We weren't talking to you, Erin," May said, rolling her eyes. Erin was always bragging. Secretly, the Pony Tails thought Erin's parents bought her things because Erin whined so much. That was one reason the Pony Tails didn't like her. Another reason was that Erin was a goody-goody. She always tried to impress teachers and other adults, even if it meant being a tell-tale.

Erin stuck her tongue out at May. "It's a free country," she said. "I can talk about anything I want."

"Just ignore her," Jasmine whispered to her friends. She didn't like to make trouble.

"I heard that," Erin said, glaring at Jasmine. "You think you're so great. But you're not. Your parents won't even buy you a stupid toy horse."

Jasmine's face turned red, but she didn't say anything.

May frowned at Erin. "You'd better shut up," she warned.

"Don't tell me what to do, May," Erin said.

"Why shouldn't she?" Corey said. "After all, it's a free country."

May and Corey laughed at the angry look on Erin's face, but Jasmine didn't join in. She hated fighting. She didn't like Erin any more than her friends did, but she wished they could just be nice to each other.

Erin tossed her head, making her long blond hair bounce around her shoulders.

"You three had better watch out," she said. "You always act like you're better than everyone else. Just because you have your own ponies, that doesn't make you anything special. You'd just better watch out." Erin didn't have her own pony the way Jasmine, May, and Corey did. She rode one of Pine Hollow's schooling ponies, a peppy Appaloosa named Quarter.

"Don't worry about her," Corey whispered to Jasmine. "She's all talk and no action. She wouldn't dare do anything to us."

Jasmine wasn't so sure about that. She had seen the look on Erin's face — and she was afraid that Erin wanted to make trouble for the Pony Tails.

2
MAX'S BIG
ANNOUNCEMENT

A few minutes later Max started the Pony Club meeting the way he always did – by saying, "Horse Wise, come to order!"

All the riders stopped talking and turned to listen. Jasmine sat up straight as she waited to hear what Max would say.

"You're probably wondering what

we'll be doing today," Max said. "Well, I won't keep you in suspense. We're going to talk about equitation. Who knows what that means?"

Several riders raised their hands. Max pointed to an older girl with light brown hair named Lisa Atwood. Lisa was a member of The Saddle Club. That was a group made up of three older riders in Horse Wise. Just like the Pony Tails, the members of The Saddle Club were best friends who loved riding.

"Equitation is another word for riding," Lisa said. "In equitation classes at horse shows, the judges score a rider's skills rather than those of her horse."

"That's right," Max said. "To be good at equitation, a rider has to be in full control of herself and the horse. I'm going to have you practise your equitation as a big sister-little sister project for this week. At next week's

14

meeting, we'll have an informal competition, complete with rosettes, to see what we've learned." He waited for the excited chatter to die down, then continued. "At the end of this meeting you'll be assigned partners to work with on your equitation. You can hold your first practice session right away. You should concentrate on flat work, with a little bit of simple jumping if you have time."

Jasmine, May, and Corey exchanged excited glances. They liked working with the older girls in Horse Wise, especially when they were paired with members of The Saddle Club. They were nice, and they knew a lot about riding.

"This project sounds like fun," Corey whispered. "I've never been in a horse show before." She hadn't been riding at Pine Hollow as long as her friends. May and Jasmine had taken part in several competitions against other other local Pony Clubs.

"I can't wait," May agreed, squirming happily. "I wonder who my partner will be?"

"I hope I get Carole," Jasmine said, as softly as she could. She glanced at Max as she spoke. She knew he hated to catch anyone whispering when he was talking. Still, when there was exciting news like this to talk about, it was hard to keep quiet.

"Me too!" May whispered back. Carole Hanson, another member of The Saddle Club, was the best rider in Horse Wise.

Erin heard them. "Don't count on it," she whispered. "Why should you three always hog the best big sisters? I want Carole to be my partner this time."

"Poor Carole," May said sarcastically. Unfortunately she forgot to whisper.

Max looked over at them and

frowned. "Do you have a question, May?" he asked.

"No," May said with a weak smile. "Sorry."

As Max continued to talk about equitation, Jasmine sneaked a glance at Carole Hanson. Carole was friendly and easy to talk to, and she knew a lot about horses. Jasmine was sure she could win a first rosette at the competition next week if she was Carole's partner. She could already picture how nice the rosette would look on the bulletin board above the desk in her room. That was where she always hung her A-plus papers and the special awards she won at school.

Suddenly Jasmine realized she hadn't been paying attention to what Max was saying. Even if she got Carole as a partner, she wouldn't win the competition if she didn't know what she was supposed to be doing. She listened carefully as Max talked about aids – signals to tell a horse what to do. He also discussed posture, mounting and dismounting, and all the other things that would be judged in an equitation class at a horse show.

"But the key word for our own little show next week is teamwork," Max said. "That and plenty of practice will be the keys to a good performance."

Jasmine, May, and Corey smiled at each other. They were good at team-work. After all, that was what the Pony Tails were all about.

3
PICKING TEAMS

Finally Max looked at his watch. "That's it for today," he said. "I'll assign the teams. Then you can get together and start practising."

Before Max could go on, Erin raised her hand.

"Yes, Erin?" Max said.

"I'd like to be Carole Hanson's partner," Erin announced in the polite voice she always used when talking to adults. "Please? I just know she and I would work very well together."

"Thanks for your enthusiasm, Erin," Max said with a smile. "And I'm sure Carole is flattered. But I'll be drawing the names out of a hat. That will make things fair for everyone."

"Oh." Erin lowered her hand and sat back, pouting just a little.

May couldn't believe Erin's nerve. How dare she just raise her hand and request to be paired with the best rider in the group!

"She sounded like she thought she was just going to get exactly what she wanted, just because she asked," Corey said quietly.

"I know," May whispered. "She's like that at school, too. The problem is, she usually gets away with it there." The three friends were all in different classes at Willow Creek

20

Junior School. Erin was in May's class. "The teachers all love her," May added.

Corey glanced over at Max. "Shhh," she said. "He's getting ready to pick the names." She crossed all the fingers on both her hands. "I hope I get someone good!"

Max was holding two hard hats, each filled with little slips of paper. He pulled a slip out of one of the hats and read it. "The first little sister is Corey Takamura," he announced.

Corey let out a squeak of excitement and crossed her arms for an extra bit of luck. She held her breath and waited.

Max picked a slip from the other hat. "Corey, your big sister is . . . Lisa Atwood!"

Corey let out her breath in a big whoosh and smiled. She saw Lisa waving at her from across the room and waved back happily.

"Lucky you," May said. They all knew that Lisa was a very good rider and a smart and patient teacher. Being paired with her was almost as good as being paired with Carole.

Max called a few more pairs as May and Jasmine waited eagerly for their own names. "Maybe we'll end up with Carole and Stevie," Jasmine whispered. Stevie Lake was the third member of The Saddle Club. She was another favourite of the younger girls because of her good sense of humour.

But a moment later Max announced that Stevie would be working with Jessica Adler. Jessica hadn't been riding at Pine Hollow very long, so the Pony Tails didn't know her well. But they liked her and were glad she had a good partner.

"May Grover!" Max called at last.

"Carole, Carole, Carole," May chanted under her breath.

But when Max looked at the next slip of paper, he announced, "May, you'll be working with Veronica."

May groaned. Veronica diAngelo was a good rider, but she was also a spoiled, nasty rich girl. She never did any work around the stables if she could help it, and she hardly ever bothered to talk to the younger riders.

"Too bad," Corey said, patting May's arm.

"Maybe being partners with Veronica won't be horrible," Jasmine pointed out. "She's a pretty good rider."

"I suppose so," May said, looking uncertain. "But she's a pretty bad teacher. I'll just have to work extra-hard and hope for the best."

Most of the other pairs were assigned by the time Max called Jasmine's name.

"Cross your fingers," Corey urged

her friend. "You might still get Carole."

"Or I might get Simon," Jasmine said. The only older riders left were Carole and Simon Atherton, a clumsy, nerdy boy who was a less experienced rider than most of the younger students. Jasmine watched anxiously as Max pulled another slip. "OK, Jasmine," he said. "You and Carole will be partners this time."

"Yay!" Jasmine cheered.

Erin frowned at her. "It figures," she snapped "You may think you have all the luck, Jasmine, but it won't last. I'll make sure of that."

"Erin!" Max called. "Pay attention. You're the last name in this hat." He read the last slip in the other hat. "Your partner is Simon."

Simon waved cheerfully at the younger girl. "Hi there, Erin," he called. "Looks like I'm your big sister for the week."

Most of the other students laughed, but Erin frowned and shot Jasmine a dirty look. "Just remember what I said, Jasmine," she muttered. "And don't say I didn't warn you."

4
JASMINE'S CELEBRATION

When Jasmine got home from Pine Hollow that evening, she was still worrying about Erin's threat. May and Corey had told her to forget about it, but Jasmine had hardly been able to concentrate on anything Carole had said during their first practice.

Jasmine went upstairs and down the long hall to her mother's studio at the back of the house. Mrs James was an artist and worked at home. Opening the door quietly, Jasmine saw that her mother was working at a table by the window. The last few rays of the setting sun came in through the skylight in the ceiling, shedding a rosy glow over the big room.

Mrs James looked up and smiled when she heard her daughter come in. "Hello, Jasmine," she said. "How was Pony Club today?"

"OK," Jasmine said. She walked over and perched on a stool near the table. Mrs James had just finished weaving a wall hanging on her big loom. Now she was clipping off loose threads with a small pair of scissors. "That looks nice," Jasmine said. "The colours are really pretty."

"Thanks." Mrs James smiled and then snipped off one more thread. Then she set her scissors down, stood, and stretched. "Whew! I didn't realize how late it was getting," she said. She sniffed the air. "I don't smell any dinner cooking. That must mean your father is still in his study. I guess he got caught up in his work, too."

Mr and Mrs James took turns cooking dinner for the family. Jasmine's father worked for an environmental company. He had an office in nearby Washington, D.C. He also had a small study in the basement where he often worked at the weekend. Jasmine didn't mind that both her parents worked so hard, since it never stopped them from spending lots of time with her.

"So what's going on at Pine Hollow?" Mrs James asked as she and Jasmine headed downstairs to start dinner.

Jasmine shrugged. "We're studying equitation," she said. "We're supposed to practise all this week, and

29

then Max is going to give out rosettes next week at Horse Wise. Carole Hanson is my partner."

"Isn't that the girl who's such a good rider?" Mrs James said. "You must be happy about that."

"I am, sort of," Jasmine said slowly. "But Erin Mosley wanted to be Carole's partner. Now she says she's going to make me sorry I was so lucky."

Mrs James frowned. "That's not very kind of her," she said. "But you shouldn't worry, Jasmine. There's not much Erin can really do about it, is there?"

Jasmine shrugged again. "I'm not sure," she muttered. "She's pretty nasty."

"It won't help anyone for you to be nasty in return," Mrs James pointed out as they entered the cheerful yellow-and-blue painted kitchen. "All you can do is try to be nice."

"I suppose you're right," Jasmine said with a sigh. It sounded so easy when her mother said it. Mrs James was nice to everyone – and everyone was nice to her. Maybe her method *did* work. "I suppose I can try to be nice to Erin."

"That's the spirit," her mother said with a smile. "I'm proud of you. And I don't just mean for this, Jasmine. You're really growing up, you know."

"I am?" Jasmine said, taking the lettuce her mother handed her and washing it in the sink.

Mrs James nodded. "You're getting more independent all the time," she said. "I think May and Corey have been a good influence. They're both such strong girls. Pine Hollow has been good for you, too." She walked over and patted her daughter on the shoulder. "But most of the credit goes to you, Jasmine. You're really becoming your own person."

31

Jasmine wasn't sure why her mother was making such a big deal out of being proud of her, but she didn't mind. "Thanks, Mum," she said.

"I have an idea," Mrs James said, pausing on her way to the pantry. "Why don't we do something to celebrate? Say, a special dinner with all your favourite foods."

"You mean tonight?" Jasmine said doubtfully, glancing at the clock on the wall.

Mrs James laughed. "Well, maybe not," she agreed. "Tonight we'd better stick with something quick. How about next Saturday? That will give me time to do some shopping. I'll make my special vegetable lasagna, and your father can bake those molasses-oatmeal biscuits you like."

"That sounds great," Jasmine agreed. "If I win a rosette, we can celebrate that, too."

32

"Sure," Mrs James agreed. "But you don't have to win a rosette for your father and me to be proud of you. I've been looking for an extra-special way to tell you that. Next week will be the perfect time."

They continued making dinner in friendly silence. Jasmine thought over what her mother had said about shopping. At first Jasmine had thought she meant grocery shopping. But now she wondered. Could her mother be planning to shop for something else, something extra-special? Something like . . . a model pony?

The more she thought about it, the more certain Jasmine became. Her mother was going back to the shopping centre to buy her the model pony! Now Jasmine wouldn't have to wait until Christmas. She already knew what she was going to name her new pony: Outlaw Junior. She couldn't wait to tell her friends.

*   *   *

After dinner Jasmine hurried next door to Corey's house. She found Corey and May in Corey's stables, leaning over a large cage in one corner.

"Come and look at these babies," May called as soon as she saw Jasmine. "They're so cute!"

Corey's mother was a veterinarian who took care of all sorts of small animals. She sometimes used one part of their barn to house her patients. Corey's pony, Samurai, and a baby goat named Alexander lived in the other part. Samurai was poking his head over his stall door, trying to see what the fuss was about.

Jasmine wanted to know, too. She hurried over to the cage. Inside was a floppy-eared rabbit with eight squirming babies around her. "Oh!" she exclaimed, dropping to her knees next to her friends. "They're adorable."

"They were born a few weeks ago," Corey said. "The owner dropped them off yesterday — she wants Mum to take care of them while she's away."

"Can we pet them?" Jasmine asked.

"Go ahead," Corey said. "The mother is tame. See?" She reached carefully into the cage and stroked the mother rabbit's soft fur.

"I can't believe how many babies there are," Jasmine said. She gingerly reached in and touched one of the fuzzy little creatures.

"Can you imagine having that many brothers and sisters?" May said. "What a nightmare!" May was always fighting with her two older sisters, Ellie and Dottie.

"Oh, I don't know," Jasmine said thoughtfully, still gently petting the mother rabbit. "I don't think I'd mind."

"Me neither," Corey agreed.

May rolled her eyes. "You're both only children. You have no idea what you're talking about. Sisters are nothing but trouble."

"Maybe your sisters are a pain sometimes," Jasmine said. "But at least you're never lonely. Besides, Ellie and Dottie can be really nice sometimes. Remember how they threw you that surprise birthday party?"

"That was a once-in-a-lifetime event," May declared. "Believe me, I'd be happy to give away one of my sisters to each of you, if only my parents would let me."

Corey giggled. "No thanks. But I still think it would be nice to belong to a big family like the one Mrs Rabbit has."

After a few minutes of watching the rabbits, Jasmine remembered why she had come to find her friends.

She told them everything her mother had said. "I think she's going to buy me the pony," she finished.

"That's great," Corey said. "I can't wait to see it."

"Your mum's right about Erin, you know," May added. "There's really nothing she can do to you. Especially since she wouldn't dare do anything to get herself in trouble with Max."

Jasmine sighed. "I hope you're right."

"She is," Corey said firmly. "You can't waste your time worrying about Erin. It'll just get in the way of learning what you're supposed to be learning."

"I hope I can learn what *I'm* supposed to learn this week," May said, looking glum. "I can tell Veronica diAngelo isn't going to be much help. Today she just ignored me and rode Danny around and around the ring."

"It's too bad you got stuck with her," Corey said.

May shrugged. "I'm just glad you two got good partners. You're going to have fun."

"Unless Erin finds a way to ruin it," Jasmine said darkly.

"You can't let her," Corey said. "The worst thing you can do is worry so much that you can't concentrate on equitation."

"That would play right into Erin's sneaky little hands," May pointed out. "See? You just *have* to ignore her."

Jasmine smiled. Her friends were making her feel better. After all, what could Erin really do to her? "You know something May?" Jasmine said, reaching in to give the mother rabbit another pat. "You're right. I'm not going to worry about Erin!"

5
ERIN'S REVENGE

The next practice session was on Tuesday after school. When the Pony Tails arrived, they found Carole and Lisa waiting for them. Veronica was nowhere in sight.

"Oh, well," May said. "It looks like I'm on my own."

"You can ride with us if you want," Carole offered. "You don't mind, do you, Jasmine?"

"The more the merrier," Jasmine said. She was glad. It would be easier to ignore Erin with May around. Carole and Lisa went inside to tack up their horses, and the younger girls headed toward the stalls of the ponies they would be riding that day. The three girls rode Pine Hollow ponies for their weekday lessons.

Jasmine and May led Peso and Dime to the outdoor ring. Carole was waiting for them on her horse, a pretty bay gelding named Starlight. Max had assigned each pair of students their own practice space. There was a schooling ring and paddock in the front of the stables, other paddocks and rings scattered around the grounds, and larger fields and meadows. May and Veronica had been scheduled for the indoor ring in the centre of the stable building. It was a great place to ride during bad weather, but on a breezy spring day like this one, May was happy to be outdoors.

"I hope Erin doesn't try to cause trouble today," Jasmine said as she opened the gate and led Peso through.

"Don't worry," May said. "I haven't seen her yet. Maybe she's not going to show up at all."

Just then the girls heard a familiar whining voice. "Carole, could you come here for a minute?"

May and Jasmine turned and saw that Erin had just come out of the barn leading Quarter, the pony she usually rode. The reins of his bridle were twisted and knotted.

Carole glanced over and dismounted. "I'll be right there," she called. "May, could you watch Starlight for a minute?"

"OK," May said. She took Starlight's reins in her free hand and gazed up at the tall horse. He looked back down at her calmly.

41

Jasmine watched Carole and Erin. Carole was speaking to Quarter soothingly as she tried to untangle the reins. Erin was watching with her arms folded across her chest and a satisfied look on her face.

A moment later Simon Atherton appeared in the stable doorway, leading a gentle horse named Patch. "What's going on out here?" he asked when he saw Carole with Quarter. "Are you having some trouble with your horse, Erin?"

"He's a pony, not a horse," she replied. "And don't worry. Carole's taking care of it."

"Actually," Carole said, "Simon could probably help you with this, Erin. He is your big sis— er, big brother, after all." She showed Simon the problem. "All you have to do is untangle this mess."

"No problem," Simon said, starting to work.

Carole returned to the ring and took back Starlight's reins. "Sorry about that, you two," she said. "Now let's get started."

Fifteen minutes later Jasmine had almost forgotten about Erin. She, May and Carole were hard at work practising turning. Carole explained that it was easy to turn incorrectly if you didn't guide the horse or pony with the proper aids. She demonstrated by asking Starlight to make some awkward turns.

"Now that you've shown us the wrong way, are you going to show us the right way?" May asked.

Carole laughed. "Just watch," she said. "Pay close attention to what I'm doing with my legs. Your legs and seat are more important than your hands when you're turning. And watch the way my hips and shoulders stay in line with Starlight's body."

Jasmine and May watched as Carole and Starlight smoothly turned left, then right, then in a graceful figure eight. They started out at a walk, then moved to a trot. Finally Carole brought the gelding to a clean stop in front of the other girls.

"That was great, Carole," Jasmine said admiringly. "I wish I could ride like that." It was clear that Carole was in complete control of her horse.

"You will someday, Jasmine," Carole said. "All it takes is practice and concentration. Oh, and being horse-crazy doesn't hurt."

"Well, we've got that part down already," May declared. All three girls laughed.

"Why don't you two try turning now?" Carole suggested. "I'll watch and give you hints. Jasmine, you go first."

Jasmine nodded and signaled for Peso to walk. Just as she was about to turn him, she heard a loud, whiny voice.

"Carole," Erin called. She was leaning on the gate. "We're having some trouble getting Quarter to back up. He won't do it no matter what I do. Could you come see if you can tell what's wrong with him?"

Carole furrowed her brow. "Quarter won't back up? That's not like him." She looked at Jasmine and May and shrugged. "This should only take a minute," she said. "Do you mind?"

Jasmine and May shrugged in return and watched as Carole rode out of the ring.

"I suppose that's the trouble with being the best rider at Pine Hollow," Jasmine said. "Everyone always wants your help."

May narrowed her eyes. "I don't think that's the whole story here," she muttered.

"What do you mean?" Jasmine asked.

"I think Erin is doing this on purpose. She's never had any trouble getting Quarter to back up before," May said. "Isn't it kind of strange she suddenly needs Carole to help her now?"

"Not really," Jasmine said. "Everyone has bad days – riders *and* ponies. Maybe Quarter is just feeling a little stubborn today."

"Maybe," May said. "Or maybe not." She gathered Dime's reins and signaled for him to trot. "Come on," she told Jasmine. "We might as well keep practising until Carole gets back."

A few minutes later Jasmine and May saw Carole leading Starlight toward the paddock gate. "Quarter seems all right now," she called to Erin.

"Wait," Erin called back. "While you're here, can I ask you one more thing?"

Jasmine and May saw Carole glance at them, then back at Erin. Then she turned Starlight around and headed back towards Erin. Soon the two were deep in conversation. Every once in a while, Erin pointed to her stirrups.

"I wonder what she's asking her now," Jasmine said.

"I don't know," May replied with a little frown. She slid down off Dime's back and stood staring at the paddock, her hands on her hips. "She's probably getting Carole to explain how to mount or something."

Jasmine bit her lip. She wanted to believe that nothing unusual was going on, but May wasn't helping. "Don't you think you're being a little too suspicious?"

"Nope," May said. "The trouble was,

I wasn't being suspicious enough before. I didn't think Erin would go through with her threat because she'd be afraid Max would find out. But she's even sneakier than I thought."

"What do you mean?" Jasmine asked. "She's not really doing anything wrong."

"Exactly," May said with a nod. "It's the perfect revenge. She's making sure she ruins your chance to work with Carole without letting anyone know she's doing it – not even Carole."

Before Jasmine could answer, Carole returned to the ring. "Sorry about that," she said. "Erin was having trouble with her stirrups. Now, where were we?"

"You were going to watch us turn and tell us what we're doing wrong," May reminded her. "Jasmine was just about to start."

"Right," Carole said. "Go ahead, Jasmine."

Jasmine took a deep breath and rode Peso around the ring, paying extra attention to how she was sitting while her pony turned.

"That's good," Carole called to her. "But loosen the inside rein a little more. That's right. See? Now his head is free to look where he's going. Don't let your outside leg swing. And make sure he knows you're in control."

Jasmine tried to do everything Carole said. Before long she could tell she and Peso were doing much better.

"Carole!" Erin's voice ruined Jasmine's concentration once again. She frowned and quickly brought Peso to a stop. She looked over and saw that Erin was at the gate, waving to get Carole's attention.

"What is it, Erin?" Carole asked patiently.

"I just remembered one more thing I wanted to ask you," Erin said. "How can I get Quarter to lengthen his stride? I asked Simon, but he has no idea."

May shot Jasmine a look. Jasmine started chewing on her lower lip again. This time she had to admit that May might be right. Jasmine was sure it was true that Simon had no idea how to make Quarter lengthen his stride. But she was equally sure that Erin *did* know. They had practised that move in a lesson a few weeks earlier and Erin and Quarter hadn't had any trouble.

"Now do you believe me?" May asked, riding over to Jasmine as Carole left the ring again.

Jasmine shrugged. "I suppose so," she said. "But I don't want to tell Carole what Erin's doing. If we do, we'll be tell-tales just like she is."

"You're right," May agreed. "But we can't just sit here and do nothing."

"We have to," Jasmine said,

slumping down in the saddle. "Face it, May. Erin has us beaten this time."

The rest of the day's practice went the same way. Every time Jasmine and May seemed to be learning something, Erin came over and interrupted. After the lesson on lengthening Quarter's stride, Erin needed help with changing leads. Then she was afraid there was some-thing wrong with Quarter's bit. Then Simon fell off and Carole had to help catch Patch. Jasmine was pretty sure that last part was just a coincidence, but May wasn't.

"I bet she's a witch, and she put a curse on him to make him fall," May said. Jasmine couldn't tell if May was kidding or not.

Jasmine was almost relieved when the practice was over. She had learned a little bit. For one thing, she was much more confident about making simple turns. But she knew that wouldn't be enough to win her a rosette on Saturday. More importantly, she knew she was not getting a fair chance to learn from Carole. It was very frustrating. Still, there didn't seem to be anything she could do about it.

After she had groomed Peso, Jasmine went outside and found Corey and May. Corey had been working with Lisa in a paddock behind the stables, so Corey hadn't seen Erin's sneaky tricks. May was telling her about them.

Just then Jasmine's mother pulled her car into the drive. The three girls piled into the back seat. They always sat together that way, even though their parents joked that it made them feel like chauffeurs.

"Hi, girls," Mrs James said. "How was the practice?"

"Terrible," May announced, at the

same time that Jasmine and Corey said, "Fine."

Mrs James laughed. She was used to May's strong opinions. Usually she liked to hear all about them. But today she didn't say anything else as she turned the car toward home.

"What are we going to do about Erin?" May asked.

"I don't think we should do anything," Jasmine said. "I thought we'd already decided that."

"I agree with Jasmine," Corey said. "Unless we want to be tell-tales just like Erin, we can't tell Carole or Max what she's doing. Maybe Carole will work it out on her own."

"Maybe she won't," May said. "She's always so glad to answer everybody's questions about horses. She might not notice that Erin is suddenly asking more than usual."

"At least not until it's too late," Jasmine murmured, thinking of the

53

imaginary first rosette above her desk.

Corey looked at Jasmine sadly. "It's not fair," she said. "Erin shouldn't be able to ruin this for you." She glanced forwards at Mrs James. Jasmine's mother was usually very supportive and understanding when any of the girls had a problem. Corey was a little surprised that she didn't seem to be paying attention to their conversation.

Jasmine was surprised at her mother's behaviour, too. She wondered if her mother thought Jasmine was so grown up that she didn't need help any more. She hoped not.

"I suppose I'll just have to hope that tomorrow's practice goes better," she said with a sigh.

May and Corey nodded. They hoped so, too.

6
JASMINE HEARS SOMETHING TERRIBLE

The next day the younger riders had their normal Wednesday riding lesson. The older riders started to arrive for equitation practice as the lesson ended. Carole, Stevie, and Lisa arrived together and waved at their little sisters. May was just about to ask Carole if she could ride with her and Jasmine again when Veronica strolled past the ring, heading for the stables.

Max looked surprised to see her. "Hello, Veronica," he said. "You're right on time."

"On time for what?" Veronica said. "We don't have a lesson today. I just dropped by to pick up my sweater."

"Don't tell me you've forgotten," Max said. "Your big sister duties are waiting. You're supposed to get together with your partner today."

Veronica frowned. "Oh, that," she said. "Um, I don't think my partner is here. So I don't think I'll stick around."

"I'm right here, Veronica," May announced, riding forward.

Max smiled. "You'd better go and tack up Danny," he told Veronica firmly. "I'll expect you in the indoor ring in ten minutes."

Veronica looked annoyed, but she knew better than to argue with Max when he used that tone. She stomped into the stable without another word. May rolled her eyes and followed.

Corey giggled. "Poor May," she said. "She's going to have her hands full today."

Jasmine smiled weakly. She had a feeling that without May around today's practice was going to be even worse than yesterday's.

She was right. Erin didn't leave Carole and Jasmine in peace for more than five minutes. She made up all sorts of questions and requests for help, so that Carole had to run back and forth from ring to paddock throughout the whole practice. By the end of the hour, Jasmine was more frustrated than ever.

She didn't see either of her friends as she untacked Peso. After giving the pony a good grooming, she picked up the saddle and bridle and headed for the tack room to clean them. But as she reached the door, she heard voices from inside. It was The Saddle Club – and they were talking about her!

"I'm not sure how much real progress Jasmine and I are making," Carole was saying. "In fact, it seems like we're not getting anything done at all. It's really kind of disappointing."

Jasmine's eyes widened and she shrank back against the hallway wall, hoping the older girls hadn't seen her.

"Don't worry," Lisa said to Carole. "Everyone has a bad practice once in a while."

"Lisa's right," Stevie added. "Don't let it bother you."

"I know," Carole said. "But you know how it is. It can be pretty annoying . . ."

Jasmine's eyes filled with tears. She couldn't listen any more. Clutching her tack to her chest, she raced back toward Peso's stall.

The next morning at the school bus stop, May and Corey were waiting for Jasmine impatiently. "What happened to you after we dropped you off at home yesterday?" May demanded as soon as she spotted her friend. "We waited for you. We thought you were coming to Corey's house for ice-cream."

Jasmine shrugged, not meeting her eye. "I didn't feel good," she said. "I needed to have a nap."

"Is that why you couldn't come to the phone last night?" Corey asked. "Your mum said you'd already gone to bed."

But May was looking at Jasmine through narrowed eyes. "Something happened yesterday, didn't it?" she said. "You look upset. Come on, you can tell us. Was it Erin again?"

Jasmine's eyes started to well with tears as she thought back to yesterday. She just shook her head. She was afraid she would start to cry if she tried to speak.

Corey looked worried. "It's OK, Jasmine," she said gently, putting an arm around her friend's shoulders. "We just want to help."

"It – it's Carole," Jasmine said at last. "She doesn't like me."

"What?" May looked surprised. "What makes you say that? Of course she likes you."

Jasmine shook her head. "I overheard her talking to her friends," she explained. "She thinks I'm a terrible rider. She even said I was annoying."

Corey gasped. "You must have heard her wrong."

"I didn't," Jasmine insisted. "She said we weren't making progress, and it was really annoying. She probably wishes she could work with Erin instead of me."

Corey and May tried to convince Jasmine that she must have misunderstood, but Jasmine would not be comforted. She was sure it was all her fault. Jasmine was quiet and sad during the entire journey to school, even when Corey tried to get her to talk about the model pony she was getting on Saturday.

"This is bad," May said later that morning as she and Corey stood in the hall. They had already dropped off Jasmine at Ms Elder's classroom.

"I know," Corey said. "She's really upset. But what can we do?"

"We've got to stop Erin," May said. "I wish we could just tell her what a rotten, no-good sneak . . ."

"Jasmine would never go for that," Corey interrupted.

May nodded. "I know. That's why we have to come up with a better plan."

"I wish we could find a way to let everyone see what a trouble-maker Erin really is, without looking like tell-tales ourselves," Corey commented.

May raised one eyebrow. "Hmm," she said. "You may be on to something. Maybe there's a way to do just that!"

7
MAY AND COREY TO THE RESCUE

The last practice session was scheduled for Friday after school. The Pony Tails arrived right on time and tacked up the stable ponies.

"You know what the first step is, right?" May whispered to Corey when Jasmine wasn't listening.

Corey nodded, her eyes sparkling. She couldn't wait to help put Erin in her place. Handing Nickel's reins to May, she hurried to Max's office.

He looked up as she entered. "Hello, Corey," he said pleasantly. "Ready for practice?"

"Almost," she said. "I have to ask you something, though. Um, do you think Lisa and I could practise somewhere else today?"

Max looked surprised at the request. "Why?"

"Well, that tree next to the back paddock is blooming, and I think I'm allergic," Corey explained earnestly, careful to keep a straight face. "I keep sneezing."

"Of course," Max said. "I didn't realize you had allergies, Corey. Why haven't I heard about this before?"

Corey thought fast. "Well, I usually take medicine so it doesn't bother me. But my prescription just ran out and my mum hasn't had a chance to take me to the doctor for another one. I have an appointment next week," she added quickly. "So it's just a problem for today."

"I see," Max said. "Well, I haven't seen Veronica yet, so the indoor ring is probably free. You and Lisa can ride there if Veronica doesn't show up, and Lisa can work with May, too."

"Oh," Corey said. "Um, I can't ride there, either. You see, it gets too dusty since it's inside. And that bothers my—"

"Allergies," Max finished for her. He crossed his arms. "Where exactly *can* you ride with these allergies of yours?"

Corey felt her face turning red. She was afraid Max was beginning to get suspicious. "Um – in the front paddock?" she said hesitantly. "You know, where Simon and Erin have been practising. It's not too dusty, and it's away from all the trees and stuff."

"Fine," Max said with a shrug. "Tell

Simon and Erin they can move to the indoor ring."

"Great," Corey said, letting out a sigh of relief. "Thanks, Max."

Erin wasn't happy about moving, but she did as Max said. May and Corey exchanged high fives as they rode into the front paddock.

"Maybe we won't have to do anything else," Corey said hopefully, glancing over at the ring where Carole and Jasmine were warming up.

"Don't count on it," May said grimly. "I don't think Erin will give up that easily. She's pretty sneaky. We'll just have to make sure we're even sneakier." Then Lisa joined them and they had to stop talking.

Only a few minutes had passed when Erin appeared at the stable entrance. "Yoo-hoo! Carole!" she called. "There's a phone call for you. It's your father."

66

"I wonder what he wants," Carole said, glancing at her watch. "He should still be at work." She handed Starlight's reins to Jasmine and hurried inside.

Jasmine sighed. She had noticed that Erin wasn't in the nearby paddock any more, and she had hoped that meant today's practice would be better. But it looked as though it would be just as bad as the others.

Carole reappeared a moment later, looking perplexed. "There must have been some misunderstanding," she said as she remounted. "My dad wasn't on the phone. In fact, I called his office and he's not even there. His secretary said he's in a meeting."

Meanwhile Corey and May were watching the whole scene. "We missed that one," May said. "We'll have to be more careful from now on."

They soon got their chance. Erin hurried out of the building again, calling for Carole. "Max wants to speak to you," she told the older girl breathlessly. "He said it's really important."

Before Carole could respond, May slid off her pony and tossed the reins to Lisa. "Don't worry, Carole. I'll go and see what he wants," she volunteered cheerfully.

Erin scowled at her. "He asked for Carole," she said pointedly.

"Don't worry," May said again. "I'll check it out." Without waiting for an answer, she hurried past Erin and headed for Max's office.

Max was there doing some paperwork. "What are you doing here, May?" he asked. "Shouldn't you be practising?"

"Erin Mosley said you needed to talk to Carole Hanson right away," May explained innocently. "But Carole's busy, so I offered to come and see what you wanted."

Max looked confused. "I didn't ask for Carole."

"Really?" May raised her eyebrows, trying to look surprised. "That's funny. Erin was very sure about it. She said Carole had to come right away."

Max shook his head. "I have no idea what that's about," he said firmly. "Now you'd better get back out there. Did Veronica ever show up?"

"Nope," May said. "But that's OK. I'm practising with Corey and Lisa." She hurried back outside just in time to hear Erin whining at Carole to come and help her set up some jumps.

"I just saw Red inside," May said quickly, loudly enough for Carole to hear. Red O'Malley was the head stablehand. "He didn't look too busy. I'm sure he'd help you."

"Good idea," Carole said, looking relieved.

69

Erin just frowned at May and went back inside. But she returned a few minutes later. "Carole, we need your help," she called. "One of the cats is in the ring and we can't catch her." Pine Hollow was home to a number of stable cats. They usually stayed out of the horses' way, so Corey had a feeling that this particular cat hadn't wandered into the indoor ring by itself.

"I have a better idea," Corey sang out. "Why doesn't Lisa go? I heard she's the best cat-catcher in the stable because of Prancer."

It was true. The horse Lisa usually rode, a Thoroughbred named Prancer, was afraid of cats. That meant Lisa had plenty of practice getting them out of sight.

"Yes, I'll go," Lisa said good-naturedly. "No cat in the place is a match for me."

"Um, can't Carole do it?" Erin insisted.

"Better have Lisa help you this time," Carole called back. "I can't even make my own cat behave."

Erin frowned and led Lisa inside as Corey and May did their best to stifle their giggles.

After that, Corey and May managed to foil Erin at every turn. First May offered to help Erin drag the mounting block into the ring. Then Corey told Erin to ask Max's mother, Mrs Reg, for help fixing a worn-out stirrup leather. When Erin returned to ask Carole for help with jumping, Red happened to be walking by. May convinced him to help Erin, and she also made sure he knew about all Erin's other requests. Just as May had hoped, Red volunteered to help Erin and Simon for the rest of the practice. May and Corey exchanged secret grins. Erin was trapped. With Red there, she had no reason to keep running to Carole for help. They had won!

Jasmine was only vaguely aware of what was going on. She was too busy concentrating on her riding to pay much attention to Erin. Practice was going just the way she had hoped it would. Carole helped Jasmine practise and refine her hand, leg, and seat aids until Jasmine thought she could do them in her sleep. Jasmine loved every minute of it. The only thing that kept the session from being perfect was that she couldn't forget what Carole had said about her on Wednesday. But that just meant that Jasmine had to prove to Carole that she wasn't annoying or a bad rider. She had to prove she was the best little sister Carole could hope for.

8
THE EQUITATION COMPETITION

On Saturday Jasmine woke up feeling cheerful. Thanks to Friday's practice, she was confident that she would do well at today's competition, even if she hadn't practised enough to win a rosette.

Her parents had left early on an errand, promising to show up at Pine Hollow in time for the competition.

As soon as she finished breakfast, Jasmine hurried over to May's house. May and Corey were already busy loading May's pony, Macaroni, into her father's horsebox. Then the girls loaded Samurai and Outlaw on to the box, too. Jasmine, May, and Corey piled into the cab with Mr Grover for the short ride to Pine Hollow.

The next hour passed in a blur as all the young riders hurried to get ready for the competition. Finally it was time. The riders gathered with their horses and ponies near the outdoor ring. Dozens of Horse Wise family members were seated in the stands. Corey waved to her parents, who were sitting together even though they were divorced. She was glad they were both there.

May's parents and sisters were there, too. She looked around but she didn't see Mr and Mrs James. "Where

are your mum and dad, Jasmine?" she
asked.

Jasmine scanned the stands
anxiously. "I don't know. They went
off somewhere this morning, I'm not
sure where. But they said they'd be
here to watch me ride."

Just then May pointed to the fam-
iliar green car pulling into the drive.
"Here they come," she announced.
"Just in time."

"I wonder what Erin's parents look
like," Corey said.

"I don't think they're here," May
replied. "I've seen them at school a
few times. They always seem really
busy – maybe they didn't have time to
come."

The girls turned to listen as Max
stepped into the centre of the ring and
cleared his throat. "Thank you all for
coming today," he began. "These
riders have been working hard all
week, and now we're going to see

what they've learned. I want to stress that this is an informal show. That means I make up my own rules." He smiled. "And that means that I've decided to judge these teams as just that – teams. Instead of each rider performing individually, they'll enter the ring in pairs and perform each move together."

May gasped. Most of the teams seemed pleased at the news, but she was dismayed. "Veronica and I have hardly practised together at all," she whispered to her friends.

"I'm sure Max will know whose fault that is," Corey said, trying to make her friend feel better. "Anyway, at least Veronica can ride. Just think about Erin and Simon!"

That did make May feel a little better. Simon was a terrible rider, and because Erin had been so busy trying to distract Carole, she and Simon had practised together even less than May and Veronica had.

Max began calling the riders into the ring two by two. He had each pair perform a set of simple moves, including stopping, starting, backing up, walking, and doing a rising and a sitting trot.

Jasmine waited anxiously as the first few pairs went, feeling more and more nervous all the time. She really wanted to do well and prove to Carole once and for all that she was a good rider. Finally Max called their names.

"Let's do it," Carole said, giving Jasmine an encouraging smile as she urged Starlight forward. Jasmine smiled back and followed.

When they left the ring a few minutes later, Jasmine was smiling even harder. Their performance had been almost flawless. They had moved together perfectly as a team, thanks to Carole's careful teaching yesterday – and to the work they had managed to do earlier in the week between Erin's interruptions. Maybe a rosette wasn't out of the question after all. Glancing over, she saw her parents applauding wildly. She grinned and waved.

Once her turn was over, Jasmine was able to relax and enjoy herself. She watched proudly as Corey and Lisa turned in a strong performance. Then she crossed her fingers as May and Veronica entered the ring. They had some trouble staying together since they had hardly practised, but they were both good enough riders to squeak by.

Erin and Simon, on the other hand, were as bad as the Pony Tails had hoped. When Max said to go left, Simon went right. When he said to trot, Simon cantered. And instead of trying to help him do better, Erin just got angrier and angrier. She seemed to forget that adults were watching as she yelled and scowled at Simon. It was a relief when they finished. May and Corey traded grins as Erin rode out of the ring without even bothering to wait for Simon.

"Maybe that will teach her a lesson about improving her attitude," Corey murmured to May.

May smiled. "Even if it doesn't, she'll think twice about messing with the Pony Tails again!"

9
THE FINAL ROUND

After each team had ridden, Max stepped forward. "Great job, everyone," he said. "You're making my decision very difficult. Some teams were clearly stronger than others, but I still can't decide who deserves which of the four rosettes. So I think we need to have one more round of competition for the four finalists."

Jasmine held her breath and crossed her fingers. She saw Corey do the same thing.

"Red is going to set up the ring while I announce the final four teams," Max went on. "We'll be doing some simple jumping at a trot to pick the winners."

Jasmine gulped. Jumping? She and Carole hadn't had time to practise jumping at all. Jasmine uncrossed her fingers. Maybe it would be better if she weren't a finalist. She didn't want to mess up in front of Carole – not after the first round had gone so well.

"The finalists, in no particular order, are as follows," Max said. "Lisa and Corey, Stevie and Jessica, Adam and Amie, and Carole and Jasmine."

Cheers went up as the names were announced. Jasmine felt butterflies in her stomach. Was she ready for this?

"It will be a few minutes before the course is ready," Max said. "Those of you who aren't in this round can put your horses and ponies away. Finalists, just relax."

"Easy for him to say," Carole said to Jasmine with a smile. "He's not the one who's nervous."

Jasmine looked at the other girl. "You mean you're nervous, too?" she said in disbelief. "But you're so good! You always ride perfectly."

Carole laughed. "Come on, Jasmine," she said. "You know that's not true. Nobody always rides perfectly – not even an Olympic gold medallist. And everybody gets nervous before a competition. Especially when it's the finals!"

"Really?" Jasmine said shyly. "I thought it was just me. You know, because I'm not that good yet."

"What do you mean?" Carole said. "You're one of the best junior riders at

Pine Hollow. I was just talking about that with my friends the other day. I think we make a good team."

"Really?" Jasmine said again. She could hardly believe her ears. "Then you don't think I'm annoying?"

Carole looked surprised. "Annoying?" she repeated. "Of course not. Whatever gave you that idea?"

"I, um, heard you talking to your friends," Jasmine blurted out, blushing at the memory. "You said we weren't making any progress, and it was annoying."

"I did?" Carole furrowed her brow. Then suddenly she laughed. "Oh, I know what you must have overheard. I *did* tell my friends we weren't making progress, but I also explained to them that it was because that other girl – Erin – kept asking for help." She shrugged. "I suppose it's not fun being Simon's little sister."

"I suppose so," Jasmine said.

Obviously Carole didn't know the real reason Erin had been interrupting them, and Jasmine didn't feel like explaining it.

"And you're such a good rider that I knew we could be a great team if we only had more time to work together," Carole went on. "The fact that we didn't was what was annoying."

"Oh." Jasmine was a little embarrassed. But she was also very happy that she'd been wrong. Carole Hanson thought she was a good rider! That was the best news Jasmine had heard all week. Suddenly she wasn't quite as scared of the jump course Red was setting up.

If Jasmine thought she was happy then, it was nothing compared to what she felt a half hour later. That was when she trotted forward to let Max pin a bright blue first-place rosette on to Outlaw's bridle.

10
JASMINE'S SPECIAL DINNER

"I still can't believe I won," Jasmine said for the fifteenth time, gazing happily at the blue rosette in her hands. She was sitting in the back seat of her parents' car. Mr Grover had offered to put Outlaw in the horsebox so Jasmine could go home with her parents.

"We're very proud of you," Mr

James said. "You worked hard and it showed."

"Thanks," Jasmine said. "I'm glad Corey won second place, too. And I'm sure May will do better next time if she gets a decent partner."

"You all did wonderfully," Mrs James assured her.

"So now I suppose we have even more to celebrate tonight, don't we?" Jasmine said, thinking hungrily of her mother's famous vegetable lasagna.

"Tonight?" Mrs James said quickly, glancing at her husband. "Oh my. It's Saturday already, isn't it?"

Jasmine leaned forward, suddenly feeling less happy. "You didn't forget, did you?" she asked. "We were going to have my favourite dinner tonight."

"I'm so sorry, Jasmine," Mrs James said, turning to look at her. "I've had a lot on my mind this week, but . . . well, that's no excuse. We should have remembered our plans with you. Of course we'll still have a celebration dinner. Is it all right if I make bean burritos instead of lasagna? That's your second-favourite dinner, right?"

"Yes, that's OK," Jasmine muttered, sinking back against the seat. She couldn't believe her parents had forgotten, especially after her mother had made such a big deal about it the week before. It wasn't like them at all. They *never* forgot things like this. In fact, they lived for it. Maybe Jasmine's special day wasn't so special to them after all.

"Don't worry, pumpkin," Mr James said, glancing in the rear-view mirror. "It'll be fun, even without the lasagna."

"OK," Jasmine said. But she wasn't sure she believed it.

As soon as they got home Jasmine went out to the stables to take care of

Outlaw. For a little while she felt better as she remembered their great performance. She gave him an extra-long grooming and a handful of carrots to reward him. Then, reluctantly, she went back inside.

The burritos were almost ready. Jasmine looked around, but she saw no sign of a gift. She should have known. Not only had her mother forgotten the dinner, she'd also forgotten to buy Jasmine the model pony. Jasmine did her best to hide her disappointment from her parents as they ate, but it wasn't easy. She picked at her burrito, her appetite gone. As soon as possible, she excused herself and went to look for her friends.

She found May and Corey with the rabbit family again.

"What's wrong?" May asked as soon as she saw Jasmine. "You don't look like a happy blue-rosette winner to me."

"I don't feel like one," Jasmine said, dropping to the ground next to her friends. "My parents are acting weirdly, and I don't know why." She told them everything.

When she had finished, Corey shrugged. "It sounds like it just slipped their minds."

"That's exactly the point," Jasmine said. "That doesn't happen with my parents. They remember everything, especially when it has to do with me."

"Mine don't, that's for sure," Corey said. "I guess it's hard since they're divorced and they don't both see me all the time. Sometimes it's hard for them to keep track of everything I'm doing, especially with all the other distractions they have with work and stuff."

"Well, my parents just have two big distractions," May announced. "Ellie and Dottie."

"But my parents are different,"

Jasmine said. "Especially my mum. She always works at home, so she's always been right there whenever I needed her." Suddenly she remembered what her mother had said the other day and frowned. "I wonder if that's the problem," she said softly.

"What?" May asked.

"The other day Mum was telling me how proud she is that I'm getting more independent," Jasmine explained. She bit her lip. "Maybe she's tired of always having to take care of me. Maybe she wants me to be totally grown up so I won't bother her all the time when she's trying to work."

"I doubt that," Corey said firmly. She gestured at the rabbit family. "Even though this mother rabbit has lots of children, she still likes taking care of them all, right?"

"But she won't *always* take care of them," Jasmine pointed out sadly, watching the baby rabbits. "Someday they'll all be grown up and then they'll just have to take care of themselves." Just then she heard someone calling her name. "That sounds like Dad," she said, getting up. The three girls went outside and saw Mr James standing on his back porch.

"There you are, pumpkin," he called when he saw Jasmine. "Could you come inside? Your mother and I want to talk to you about something important."

"I'd better go," Jasmine muttered to her friends. "They probably want to yell at me or something."

"Oh, come on," May said. "I'm sure it's nothing like that."

Jasmine started walking away, dragging her feet. "Do you two want to go riding tomorrow?" she asked.

"I can't," Corey said. "I'll be with my dad. He's taking me to the Smithsonian Institute in Washington for the day."

"We're going to visit my talkative Aunt Lucy tomorrow," May said. "We'll probably be there all day."

"Rats," Jasmine said sadly. "That means if they *do* yell at me, I won't even be able to tell you about it until Monday."

A few minutes later Jasmine was sitting in the living room with her mother and father. She stared at the floor, afraid of what her parents would say to her. Her mother spoke first.

"We want to apologize again for forgetting your special dinner, Jasmine," she said. "But that's not the only thing we need to talk to you about." She paused and glanced at her husband.

"That's right, pumpkin," he said, sitting down on the settee beside Jasmine and putting his arm around her. "We have some pretty big news.

I hope you'll be as excited about it as we are."

Jasmine looked from one parent to the other. She had no idea what they were talking about. At least they didn't seem to be mad at her. "What is it?" she asked. "What's the big news?"

Her mother took a deep breath and smiled. "You're going to be a big sister, Jasmine."

"What?" For a second Jasmine didn't understand what her mother meant. Then, suddenly, she did. Her mouth dropped open in surprise. "You mean – you're going to have a baby?"

Mrs James nodded. "That's right," she said. "We just found out for certain this morning. That's where we were before your show."

"Wow," Jasmine said. "I'm going to be a big sister!" Just a few minutes ago she had been talking to her friends about brothers and sisters. And now it turned out she was going to have one herself. It didn't seem real.

"What do you think, pumpkin?" Mr James asked. "Don't be afraid to tell us. We know this kind of news takes some getting used to."

Jasmine nodded. "That's certainly right." Then she grinned. She still had lots of questions for her parents. Right now, though, all she could think about was one thing: soon there would be a new baby in the house!

11
JASMINE'S BIG NEWS

On Monday morning Corey and May arrived at the bus stop a little early. They were eager to find out how Jasmine's talk with her parents had gone. Besides that, they hadn't had a chance to talk over the details of Saturday's competition.

"Can you believe how angry Erin looked when Simon fell off in the middle of their turn?" Corey said, swinging her book bag.

May giggled. "I know. I can't believe someone could fall off Patch so often," she said. "He's the easiest horse in the whole stables to ride."

"It's too bad you got stuck with snobby old Veronica," Corey said. "Still, it was fun, wasn't it?"

"Yup," May agreed. "Even though I think I had more fun ruining Erin's revenge than I did riding." She stopped to think. "Well, maybe the *same* amount of fun. I just did better at revenge than I did at riding."

Just then Jasmine arrived. "Hi, Jasmine," Corey said. "Did everything turn out OK with your parents?"

Jasmine nodded. "They didn't want to yell at me at all. They just wanted to tell me something."

She was about to go on, but May was still thinking about Erin. "It's Erin's own fault, you know," she interrupted.

"What do you mean?" Corey asked.

"She should have known better than to mess with one of us," May said. "She knows we always stick together."

"Listen, you two," Jasmine put in. "My parents told me something rather interesting on Saturday night."

"OK," May said. "But first, you have to tell us what you did with your blue rosette. Did you hang it in your room or in the stables?"

"Actually, I haven't hung it up yet," Jasmine said. "After my parents' news, I sort of forgot about it—"

"Forgot about it?" Corey shrieked. "Are you kidding? How could you forget about a blue rosette? I hung up my red one as soon as I got home. The only problem is that now I have to win another one, so I'll have one to hang in my room at Dad's flat, too."

"That's a good idea," May agreed.

Suddenly Jasmine dropped her books on the ground and screamed at the top of her lungs. May and Corey fell silent and turned to look at her in surprise. Jasmine didn't scream very often — especially for no apparent reason.

"What is it, Jasmine?" Corey asked.

Jasmine put her hands on her hips. "Do I have your attention now?" she asked. "Good. Because I've been trying to tell you something for the last five minutes."

"Oh," May said. "Sorry. What is it?"

"It's my parents' big news," Jasmine said. She took a deep breath. "They're going to have a baby."

Corey and May gasped. "A baby!" they exclaimed in one voice.

Jasmine nodded and smiled. "My mum's pregnant. That's why she's been distracted lately."

"Wow," Corey said. "Is that why they forgot your special dinner?"

"Yes," Jasmine said. "But they both promised to try their hardest to make sure nothing like that ever happens again. They said just because there will be a new baby in the family, it doesn't mean I'm any less important to them."

"Of course not," May said. "I could have told you that."

"After I got over being excited, I started to feel a little worried, though," Jasmine admitted. "I mean, my mum was just telling me last week all that stuff about being independent. But she says that even though I'll have to be more grown up and responsible now that I'm going to be a big sister, I'll still be their little girl. And I can still count on her whenever I need her." She reached for her book bag. "Oh, and I almost forgot – we went back to the shopping centre yesterday, and they got me the model pony."

"Really?" May exclaimed. "Do you have it with you?"

Jasmine pulled a toy pony out of her bag. It was a perfect replica of Outlaw, from the white mask to the quizzical tilt of the head. "My parents said they don't usually like to celebrate by buying me things," she said. She rolled her eyes. "They call it 'encouraging materialistic values'. But they decided to make an exception this time, since we had two things to celebrate – my rosette and the new baby."

"You're so lucky you're getting a little brother or sister," Corey said, kicking at the grass along the side of the road. "That's one of the worst parts about having divorced parents. I know they're never going to have any more kids."

"You should be grateful, believe me," May said. "Sisters aren't all they're cracked up to be."

Jasmine shrugged and smiled. "I

don't know," she said. "I think it will be kind of fun to have a baby sister. I can help Mum dress her up and stuff. Or him, if it's a boy."

"It will be different for Jasmine than it is for you, May," Corey pointed out. "Jasmine will be the oldest."

"That's true," May said. "You'll get to boss the baby around, and do everything first, and get new clothes and hand them down to the baby. You're so lucky!"

Jasmine nodded slowly. She wasn't really listening to May. Instead, she was thinking about how her whole life was changing. She was going to have to learn how to be a good older sister. That was even more complicated than being a good rider. It was exciting – but a little scary, too. She knew she was going to try to be the best big sister in the world. Maybe her new brother or sister would grow up to love riding, just like Jasmine. Maybe

Jasmine would be the one to teach him or her how to ride!

The roar of the school bus interrupted her thoughts. As she climbed aboard with her friends, Jasmine glanced behind her at their little row of houses. Soon someone new would be living in one of them. That meant there were big changes ahead for all the Pony Tails – and especially for big sister Jasmine.

THE END

JASMINE'S TIPS ON HORSES' COLOURS

It took me a long time to learn the colours that people use to describe horses and ponies, because they don't always seem to make sense. It would be simple if we could just call a horse a blond, a brunette or a redhead. But horses and ponies not only have lots of colours, they also have lots of patterns. That's one of the reasons we need so many different ways to describe their coats.

First there are the solid colours. Probably the most common colour for a horse is *bay*. A bay horse has a brown coat (light, medium or dark, it's all brown) and black points. *Points* means his muzzle, tips of the ears, mane, tail and the extremeties of the four legs. But, like other ponies, they can still have white socks.

Another common colour is *chestnut*. If chestnut horses were people, most of them would be called redheads, though the colour ranges from a dark reddish brown to a light reddish brown. The ones that are the darkest and the least red are called *liver chestnuts*. That sounds like something awful a mother might make her kid eat for dinner, but my favourite pony in the whole wide world, Outlaw, is a liver chestnut, so even though it sounds funny, I love the colour. The biggest distinction between a chestnut and a bay is that a chestnut is all one colour.

A lot of horses are *grey*, too. Grey can be a solid colour or dappled. And here's the thing that I think is funny. A white horse is almost always really a grey horse. That doesn't sound as if it makes sense, but it does. If you look closely at most horses you might want to call white, you'll see that they usually have a lot of black hairs, generally on their noses and legs — and at their points. A *light grey* is one in which the white hairs predominate; an *iron grey* is one in which the amount of black is pronounced. The few real white horses are called albinos. They're like white mice and white rabbits. They've got red eyes. You don't see too many of them. I don't have a model one in my collection, either!

Sometimes you'll find a pure

black horse. The technical name for that colour coat is – you guessed it – black!

Then there are colours that are really mixes. When a colour is mixed with white, it's called a *roan*. A chestnut-and-white mix is a *strawberry roan*. A black-and-white mix is a *blue roan* and a brown-and-white mix is a *bay roan*.

Other solid colours are *palominos*. That's a golden coat (like Macaroni's) with a silvery mane. If it's a golden coat with black mane, tail and points, we call it a *dun*.

But horses don't just have colours. Sometimes they have patterns, too. Horses often have splotches of black-and-white or brown and white. If the splotches are black and white, it's a *piebald*. If they are any other colour and white, it's known as a *skewbald*. Then if it's grey and has dark splotches, it's called a *dappled grey* or, if they look like freckles, it's called a *flea-bitten grey* (I think that's a nastier name than liver chestnut!).

Then there are breeds that have distinctive patterns. The best example of that is the *Apaloosa*. Appies come in lots of different patterns, but most of them are basically white or black with black, brown, or white spots on them.

There are lots of varieties of colours and patterns, and I haven't even begun to talk about markings, but the thing I know for sure is that it doesn't matter what colour a pony is. What matters is what's in his heart. Outlaw is the most wonderful, sweetest, stubbornest, naughtiest pony in the world, and I love him to pieces.

Jasmine's tips checked by
Jane Harding, BHSAI